# Ghost Soldiers of Gandamak

J. Thomas Hennessey, Jr, PhD

# Table of Contents

# Disclaimer

This is a work of fiction. Any resemblance to actual events or individuals is coincidental.

# Introduction

This story follows two very different soldiers and their units. The first is Lieutenant James Richard Wilkinson, a member of the 44th Foot, a British Army regiment raised in 1741. Wilkinson serves as the second-in-command of the 2nd company of the Regiment, which has been in Afghanistan since 1839.

The second soldier is Lieutenant Roger Williams Short, a platoon leader in A Company, 2nd Battalion, 22nd Infantry Regiment, 1st Brigade Combat Team (BCT), 10th Mountain Division, deployed to Afghanistan in 2022.

These two young officers meet on a cold January day near a small village in northeast Afghanistan. Wilkinson, having so far survived the British brutal retreat from Kabul, finds himself among the fifty survivors forced to make a last stand on a small hilltop near the village of Gandamak. Short and 24 members of his platoon have survived the crash of their C-47 Chinook helicopter that was transporting them from their operating base west of Kabul to their departure airfield in Kandahar.

How these two young leaders and their soldiers from two different centuries struggle to survive the brutal Afghan winter and combat the relentless attacks by Afghan tribesmen illustrates the warrior spirit all soldiers possess, regardless of the years that separate them.

# Background

***LT Wilkinson's story.*** The retreat from Kabul in General Elphinstone's army included our regiment, the 44th Foot, and thousands of civilians. Many Indian servants and workers, along with a few family members, were included. From 8 January to 13 January 1842, our stretched-out line of evacuees from Kabul was repeatedly attacked by Afghan tribesmen. It was a horrendous march across some of the most challenging terrain in northeast Afghanistan, in the dead of winter. Many soldiers and civilians were lost to the continuous sniping of the tribesmen and the severe cold. Many Indians vanished in the wilderness. Our military unit, the 44th Regiment of Foot, the only surviving formation, consisting of two officers and 48 soldiers, pressed east to Jalalabad. On January 13, we found ourselves surrounded on a snowy hill near the village of Gandamak. With but 20 working muskets and two shots per weapon, the troops refused to surrender when offered that chance by the local tribal leader. A British sergeant shouted, "Not bloody likely!" when the Afghans tried to persuade us that they would spare their lives. Furious sniping began, with a series of rushes expected soon after. Had it not been for the arrival of some very strange and powerful allies, the hillock would have been overrun by tribesmen. Thus, the last survivors of a force of over 1100 of the 44th Regiment of Foot would have perished on that hillside.

# Ghost Soldiers of Gandamak

***Lt. Short's story.*** On January 12, 2022, Alpha Company, 2/22 Infantry, was scheduled to join the rest of the 1st Brigade Combat Team for redeployment to their home station at Ft Drum, New York. The remaining platoon members of Alpha Company, 30 members of the 3$^{rd}$ platoon, board a CH-47 helicopter and depart FOB Ranger. 3$^{rd}$ platoon has spent the previous 12 months as part of Operation Inherent Resolve, an operation supporting the National Afghan Army's effort to secure the northeastern region of Afghanistan. The helicopter carrying the platoon encounters severe weather and suffers a major engine failure. The helicopter attempts an emergency landing near the village of Gandamak and a Special Forces base. Unfortunately, the Chinook crashed some distance away with multiple fatalities. It is unlikely that the crew could send a distress signal, and the platoon lacks long-range communications capability. LT Short and 24 of his surviving soldiers are now an unknown distance from the Special Forces base in the middle of winter.

In this mountainous region of Afghanistan, winter days are short, nights are long, and temperatures typically hover around freezing.

# Chapter One: The Helicopter Crash Aftermath

"Lieutenant, can you hear me? How bad are you hurt?" Sergeant Wil Jackson looks at his lanky, 25-year-old platoon leader with concern. The lieutenant slowly regains consciousness and looks at his Platoon Sergeant. As many disconnected thoughts cross his mind, he asks,

"What happened, Wil? How long have I been out?"

"Lieutenant, you have been unconscious for about an hour. When the helo crashed, it was touch-and-go for our guys and the crew. We were lucky to have so many of us get out because we thought the bird would burn."

Platoon Sergeant Wil Jackson, the senior noncommissioned officer in the platoon, is relieved to see that the lieutenant is alive, alert, and unhurt except for a nasty bruise on his head. They have worked together for the past year in tough situations, and Jackson doesn't want to take over the platoon unless the lieutenant is a casualty. One thing he likes about Lieutenant Short is that the guy is well disciplined, has grown into a natural leader, and, as the troops say, "The LT knows his shit."

Jackson is the platoon sergeant that all lieutenants want and need. He knows the troops and takes care of them. He mentors the junior leaders and runs the platoon.

As Short becomes fully conscious, he immediately recalls the single largest enemy firefight the platoon experienced and asks Sergeant Jackson the obvious next question.

"OK, Platoon Sergeant, give me the bad news. How many did we lose from the platoon, and did any crew survive?"

Sergeant Jackson somberly replies, "LT, we lost five from Weapons Squad. Thankfully, the 3$^{rd}$ squad and part of the Weapons squad were on another chopper. The crew chief is still alive, but he is hurt pretty badly. He is the only injured crew member who survived. The other two crew and five of our guys caught it when the chopper went in. Without some serious medical help, I don't think the crew chief will make it. So, of the thirty members of the platoon we started with, we are down to twenty-five."

"Wil, I don't remember the crew sending distress calls before we hit. Does the crew chief know if any were sent?"

"LT, he isn't sure, but right now, we can't raise anyone on any of our frequencies, and we only have our squad radios. And these don't work long distances in the mountains anyway. So, I guess no one knows what happened to us."

"OK, Wil, let's get the troops together and find out what we have. If the rescue crews have the same weather problem as we did, it may be a long time before they find us."

"Sir, I have consolidated the remainder of the weapons squad into the first and second squads, giving each squad another couple of guys."

"Good idea, Wil. It's a good thing we all have our winter gear with us. The weather is getting colder every hour. Can we get enough of our gear from the chopper to survive for a few days?"

"Shouldn't be a problem, Lieutenant. We lost most of the troops in the forward part of the aircraft. Our gear was in the rear, and most of it survived. Since the aircraft didn't burn, there is no way for the Taliban to know we are here. They would come running if they thought an aircraft went down."

"Wil, can you have Doc come over here? I have a splitting headache."

"LT, she is on the way."

While the platoon medic, Specialist Sharon Kramer, checks out LT Short, Platoon Sergeant Jackson details the first squad leader, SGT Wilson, to collect all the platoon gear they can find from the destroyed helicopter. Wilson and his squad salvage all the M4s, two M320 mounted M4s, two M249 light machine guns, and multiple boxes of 5.56 ammunition. Two designated marksmen from the 1st and 2nd squads were able to recover their M110 7.62 sniper rifles and a container of 7.62 ammunition. No communications gear other than the three squad radios was found. They also found two cases of MREs and three cold-weather survival bags carried by every aircraft.

With a bandage on his scalp and ibuprofen for his headache, Lieutenant Short asks, "SGT Jackson, how about the rucksacks and personal gear? Did everyone manage to get theirs out of the chopper?"

"Lieutenant, most of the guys did get their rucks out, but not everyone had all they should have had in theirs."

What are we missing, Wil?"

More than anything else, I think too many troops didn't pack all their cold-weather gear. Some will be hurting depending on how long we'll be here."

"Ok, let's get the squad leaders together and work out what we need to do to remain in good shape until the rescue comes."

SGT Jackson rounds up the two squad leaders and the senior remaining member of the weapons squad, and they brush away snow and sit down on the left side of the crashed helo out of the wind.

Jackson notices that the usually calm and collected SGT Wilson, the 1st squad leader, is distressed. Wil Jackson watches Sergeant Ron Wilson continually pull on his web gear and wonders what else might be bothering him. He knows Wilson is looking forward to seeing his wife and young son, but everyone in the platoon is eager to return to Ft Drum. Jackson's experience tells him everyone reacts differently in crises, but Wilson's response is cause for concern.

On the other hand, SGT Bishop, the 2nd squad leader, seems almost blasé. Jackson wonders if Scott Bishop may be in shock because he was the nearest passenger to the five who were killed in the crash. He can't help but wonder if their differences will affect their troops. He knows everyone was looking forward to the redeployment and probably told their family and friends they would be home in a few days. It now seems it will be some time before they are found and can leave Afghanistan.

He is also concerned that Corporal Garcia, one of the remaining members of the Weapons squad, with his ordinarily olive skin now pale and sickly, appears to be in a deeper state of shock. Jackson quietly motions for Doc Kramer.

"Sharon, is there anything you can do for Garcia? He looks like he is still in shock."

"Platoon Sergeant, short of shooting him up with some stimulants, I am not sure I can help. The stimulants would wear off pretty quickly, and he would be worse off than he is now."

Ok, but check with him after this meeting and see if he needs anything."

"Wilco, top. I hate to tell you, but the crew chief didn't make it. I think even if he was medevacked, his injuries were too serious."

"I was afraid of that. Any other injuries we need to take care of?"

"Other than some cuts and bruises, everyone else is good to go."

Lieutenant Short has retrieved his map case and unsuccessfully attempted to acquire a GPS signal on his receiver. The usually reliable system for confirming the location is a concern, but it isn't something he is overly worried about, yet.

He joins the group at the side of the crashed helo out of the wind and spreads his map.

"Everyone, we have lost some great guys in the crash, and we are going to have to wait on any memorialization until after we get out of here. Since I doubt anyone knows we went down in the helo, our primary objective is to survive and get back home. I can't get a fix on our location with the GPS receiver, and the map appears to be slightly different from the terrain around us. If I remember correctly, a Special Forces camp is close to the village here (pointing to Gandamak). I would like you to review the map and then do a quick terrain study to determine how far we are from Gandamak. The SF personnel will have better radios than we do and can contact higher headquarters to let them know our location."

"Wilson, you have a question?"

"Lieutenant, what the fuck are we going to do if the Taliban finds us before our guys?"

"Well, SGT Wilson, the same thing we have been doing for the last twelve months, killing Taliban."

"But, Sir, we have no artillery or air support and now less than a platoon."

"Correct, Ron. That's why we need to get to the Special Forces camp as soon as possible. Each of you review one of the maps and give me your best estimate of where we are."

The two squad leaders and Corporal Garcia scan the map for a few minutes, then wander in different directions, each scanning the terrain around them. After thirty minutes and going out as far as a kilometer, the three returned and provided their current location estimate. While none of the three can agree on their exact location, all three agree they are south of Gandamak. They also note that there are significant elevation differences between them and the village. LT Short concurs with their assessment and issues the following order:

"Platoon Sergeant Jackson will lead a five-man patrol from $2^{nd}$ squad five to six kilometers north. Sergeant Bishop, give me five names to accompany Sergeant Jackson."

Since we don't know how far north we need to go, plan to stay on high ground so you can scope out the area to the north. We don't want to stumble on some bad guys."

"OK, Lieutenant. We have a couple of binoculars, and if we stay on the high ground, we should be able to scope out a route north to the village. Scott, have your five meet me here in ten."

While Platoon Sergeant Jackson moves out with Corporal Costanza, Specialists Crosby, Hunt, and Lambert, LT Short assembles the remaining soldiers.

## Ghost Soldiers of Gandamak

Guys, since we don't know if a distress or Mayday call was made before the Chinook crashed, our best option is to reach the Special Forces camp and contact our unit. We have some tough terrain to cross. We've done this before, and I know we can do it again. Questions? Yes, Waters?

"Sir, will we just leave the guys we lost here? They aren't even buried."

"Right now, we will cover them as best we can with material from the Chinook and available rocks. Unfortunately, I don't think we can keep any of the platoon here. If we meet up with any Taliban, we are going to need everyone available. Once we contact higher headquarters, they will recover all those from the crash."

For the next two hours, the platoon members gather material from the crashed helicopter and stones from the area. They must also scrape away almost six inches of snow to lay out and cover the eight dead. LT Short wishes he knew what to say over each of the eight mounded bodies, but finds himself unable to make any meaningful statements. He notices that many members of the platoon are still in shock. Having to carry and cover the bodies of their comrades who, just hours before, were sharing in the joy of going home, emphasizes the grimness of the situation. A gloomy and determined group of soldiers finally finishes their unwelcome task as Platoon Sergeant Jackson and his five-man patrol return.

"Lieutenant, I could barely see the village in the distance, and it is almost due north from this location in a little valley. I estimate we are about 5 to 6 kilometers away. I gotta tell you that the terrain between here and there is some of the toughest in this part of the Stan. The snow cover doesn't help either. I didn't see any activity of the Taliban, although there are a couple of places we want to be very careful for possible ambushes."

"OK, Wil. Let's get on the road so we won't be caught in the dark."

Lieutenant, we need to stay here tonight and get an early start in the morning. This also gives the folks looking for us more time to find us. A couple of the passes we must move through are tough in even low light."

"As usual, Platoon Sergeant, you have a better idea of what can or can't be done. Let's set up sentry watches and get everyone some sleep tonight."

Once Lieutenant Short and Platoon Sergeant Jackson ensured all the troops had eaten and sentry assignments were made, the two gathered in the small arctic tent and shared more than they ever thought they would.

"Lieutenant Short, I am concerned about Sergeant Wilson. His state of mind is pretty bad right now. I know he was looking forward to seeing his wife and child in the next few days. Not sure he has adjusted to the delay."

"Wil, Wilson expressed those same concerns while you were on patrol. His squad is doing all they can to cheer him up. I wonder how much difference they can make."

"Wilson is tough but a little too emotional sometimes. We may want to go easy with him until he settles down a bit."

"Let's see how well he is in the morning before we move out. Wil, how about Kramer? She doesn't seem fazed by the crash and the casualties."

Lieutenant, I don't think we give her enough credit. She is as tough as anyone in the platoon. Do you remember that first firefight? She was the first to respond to the two wounded and never flinched when the rounds were hitting all around her.

"Thanks, Wil. I hope that is one less thing we need to worry about. The only thing bothering me right now is that I'm unable to get any GPS signal. I think we know where we are, but without it, I can't be sure."

# Chapter Two: Both Units Move to Gandamak

### *3rd Platoon, A Company, 2/22 Infantry*

LT Short and the remaining members of his platoon spend the night of January 12 close to where their transport Chinook helicopter crashed. At first light, the soldiers grab some breakfast and gather their gear. LT Short and Platoon Sergeant Jackson gather the squad leaders, platoon medic, and senior corporal from weapons for a mission briefing.

"SGT Bishop, I suggest you have Costanza take the lead and make it to the farthest location during yesterday's patrol. That will be our first checkpoint. Check the map and give me a heads up when we are about half a klick from your checkpoint. SGT Wilson, you have the trail behind the command group. Corporal Garcia, your weapons squad guys will hump our additional ammo and the sixty mortar behind the platoon headquarters element. Doc Kramer, you are with SGT Jackson. I will be with SGT Bishop and the second squad. If we make contact, the second squad will lay down a base of fire, and the first squad will be the maneuver element. Garcia, the machine gunners, will fall in with the first squad. Any questions? SGT Wilson?"

"LT, we about froze our asses off last night. We must get some hot food to make it to the Special Forces camp. It might help to get a warming fire when we stop."

"SGT Wilson, I know the weather is getting colder, but the sooner we get out of here, the better off we all will be. Let's see how far we get this morning, and we may be able to do some warming and chow."

"Roger, sir, just a thought."

"Ok, let's mount up and hit the hills. SGT Bishop lead out."

As the soldiers move north through the rugged terrain, the grey, overcast sky matches their moods. This is an inhospitable land, made more so by the brutal winter weather. The snow-capped Hindu Kush Mountains in the background are not encouraging. After they have traveled for two hours, SGT Bishop calls back to LT Short,

"Lieutenant, you need to come up here and see this."

Short climbs slowly to the top of the jagged peak. He joins SGT Bishop and pulls out his binoculars. Bishop points toward the now visible village.

"Do you see them, LT?"

"I do, Bishop. Who is that, and how many do you think are in the line moving east?"

"LT, I counted about fifty total, but if you look to the north and west of the line of individuals, you can see what looks like ragheads shooting at them."

"Bishop, I can't determine what type of group is moving east. They appear to be some military unit. Can you see any better than I?"

LT, as far as I can tell, they are wearing red and blue uniforms. They seem to be gathering on the hill just south and east of the village.

"Bishop, tell the platoon sergeant to get the rest of the platoon up here as soon as possible. We may have to provide some support to a unit being attacked by the Taliban."

The undermanned platoon moves directly toward the hill now occupied by the ragtag group dressed in red and blue bedraggled uniforms.

Short sees a turban and brown-cloaked fighter with a white flag approach the hill and talk briefly with two uniformed individuals. The now prominent tribesman leaves the hill as individual shots from what appear to be muskets punctuate the otherwise still winter chill as the Americans approach.

To LT Short, this is now a group of Taliban fighters firing on them and at the group on the hill. The American soldiers return fire from their M4s and quickly suppress the musket fire. They move slowly toward the group now arranged around the hill.

LT Short calls out to a blue-clad figure on the hill, "I am Lieutenant Short, United States Army. May we assist your unit? The Taliban have fired on us, and we have engaged them. They appear to have retreated for the time being."

# Ghost Soldiers of Gandamak

## *44<sup>th</sup> Regiment of Foot, British Army*

The retreat from Kabul with the entire regiment has been a total disaster. With almost 1000 civilians dragging the pace of the march, the 44<sup>th</sup> Foot has been subjected to continuous sniping by Afghan tribesmen. The departure on January 8 was supposed to be under the protection of Wazir Akbar Khan, one of Dost Mohammad Barakzai's sons. However, all along the way, the tribesmen have proven a difficult, if not impossible, barrier to the trek to Jalalabad. By the afternoon of January 11, the regiment's remaining elements are trying to move forward and retain some order in their march. That evening, as the temperature dropped, the small fires did little to warm the soldiers or provide them with food. LT Wilkinson moves amongst the soldiers, trying vainly to lift their spirits and encourage them to eat something to maintain their strength. He reminds them that they are more than halfway to Jalalabad.

In the early morning of the 12<sup>th</sup>, the march's remnants continue eastward toward Jalalabad. By now, there are no more civilians in the column. Many have given up and returned to Kabul, and the Indian workers have disappeared. The cold and the rugged terrain make movement laborious and slow. The sniping by the tribesmen continues to take a toll. In the early afternoon, Captain Souter is wounded and unable to continue leading the survivors, so he turns over all decisions to Lieutenant Wilkinson. The rapidly dwindling number of soldiers stops for the night, attempts to warm up around small fires, and eats what little rations they have available.

## Ghost Soldiers of Gandamak

On the morning of the 13<sup>th,</sup> the regiment's survivors move toward the village of Gandamak.  Mid-morning finds the bedraggled force gathered on a small hilltop south of Gandamak. Continuous sniping by tribesmen has whittled the number of effective soldiers to 48 and 2 officers. Now in command, LT Wilkinson is approached by a tribal leader under a white flag of truce and demands to speak to the officer in command. The tribal leader gathers with LT Wilkinson and Color Sergeant Smyth and offers surrender terms.

The tribesman spokesman says, "I make this offer on behalf of the tribesmen we represent. If you surrender, we will spare your lives. If you do not surrender before the sun is lowest in the sky, we will attack and kill all of you."

Color Sergeant Smyth, a grizzled veteran of war, shouts,

"Surrender? Not bloody likely!"

Upon hearing his shout, the forty-eight soldiers scattered around the hillside, repeating his exclamation, "Not bloody likely."

LT Wilkinson, turning to the tribesmen leader, says.

"I guess you have received your answer."

"Unfortunately, Englishman, you have sealed the fate of you and your men. May Allah have pity on you."

As the tribal leader moves away and back toward his contingent, LT Wilkinson and Color Sergeant Smyth look bleakly at each other.

"Leftenant, we have but two cartridges for each weapon. After that, the bayonet will be our only defense."

"Sergeant Smyth, a bleak picture you have painted as to our continued survival."

"Aye, sir, but the lads have spoken. They know what being a prisoner of these heathen would mean."

Wounded and almost unconscious in a wagon used as an ambulance, Captain Souter calls LT Wilkinson to his side.

"Leftenant Wilkinson, should I fail in the subsequent trial, I expect that you will continue the traditions of the regiment and perform as the commanding officer."

"Captain, I hope that is not the case, but should it come to pass, you may be assured that I will carry on as the regiment demands."

Wilkinson's thoughts are suddenly interrupted by very different gunfire to the south of the hill. It is rapid and much sharper than muskets. Looking in that direction, he sees small groups of tribesmen moving quickly west and away from the hill. A strange-looking figure, clearly not a tribesman, at the head of a dispersed group of figures, approaches and calls out, "I am Lieutenant Short, United States Army. May we assist your unit? The Taliban have fired on us, and we have engaged them."

Confused, Wilkinson recognizes the different English phrases but cannot fully understand what is being said, except for 'may we provide some assistance.' He replies.

"I do not know who you are, but if you can assist us, please do so as soon as you can."

Now, alongside LT Wilkinson, Sergeant Smyth watches in amazement as twenty-five khaki-clad individuals with cloth-covered headpieces join them on the hillside. He does not recognize any of their weapons, and their curious head coverings are unfamiliar. Moreover, the amount of kit they carry is far more than that of any of his soldiers. LT Short approaches LT Wilkinson and SGT Smyth and asks,

"What is going on, and who is attacking you?"

Before LT Wilkinson can answer, SGT Smyth blurts out, "Who in the bloody hell are you bunch? You donna look like any soldiers I have ever seen."

LT Wilkinson politely turns to LT Short and introduces himself and SGT Smyth, "Leftenant Short, I am Leftenant Wilkinson of the 44th Foot of Her Majesty's army. Color Sergeant Smyth is the leading soldier in the regiment. We have traveled from Kabul and have been directed to join the garrison at Jalalabad."

LT Short replies, "I did not know that any British units were operating in this area. I could not help but notice there appear to be some wounded in your unit. Do you have a medic who is treating them? If not, we have a medic and will treat the wounded."

"Leftenant Short, we would be grateful for any medical support you can provide. Our commanding officer, Captain Souter, has been wounded and needs medical attention. After your doctor sees him, we must discuss how else you may assist."

American soldiers gather on the lower crest of the hill facing south. They are wide-eyed and struggle to understand the group they've joined. Always eager to comment on everything, Specialist Crosby asks, "Waters, just who in the hell are these people? They look like something out of an old movie set. The two wagons drawn by horses belong in a museum."

SGT Bishop replies, "Crosby, watch your mouth. These are British soldiers, and we are allies."

"But Sarge, they ain't dressed like any British outfit I have seen before. And they are carrying muskets. Can you believe that, muskets?"

At that point, a grizzled British soldier who looks like he could be 40 or 80 comes to the Americans and asks. "Who are you, lads, and where do ye come from? We havna seen your likes before."

SGT Bishop gets to his feet, approaches the British soldier, and introduces himself. "I am Sergeant Scott Bishop, squad leader in A Company, 2$^{nd}$ Battalion, 22$^{nd}$ Infantry Regiment, 1$^{st}$ Brigade Combat Team, 10$^{th}$ Mountain Division."

The British soldier withdraws his hand from a ragged mitten, grasps Sergeant Bishop's hand, and replies, "I am Corporal Sethewick, First Company, 44th Foot, and we are pleased to have some reinforcement on our way to Jalalabad. Please join us by the fire."

Sergeant Bishop gratefully accepts the invitation and joins Sethewick and two others at their small fire. Bishop looks at the three and asks, "How long have you been on the road?"

Sethewick, with a tiny bit of bread in his mouth, motions to one of the others to respond.

"I be Corporal Smithers and we have been on the march from Kabul for the past four days. The civvies and the Indians have all disappeared, and it's just us that's left. This hill was to be our last stop. And you, lads, where you be from?"

"We are stationed in New York and have been in Afghanistan for the past year. We were on our way to Kandahar for transport home when our aircraft crashed. We lost five members of our platoon in the crash. We are heading to Gandamak to link up with a special forces unit and use their radios to call for pickup."

Smithers and Sethewick look at Bishop as though he is speaking another language. Sethewick is the first to ask, "I dinna know what might be at Kandahar, but that is a long way from here. Did you call something an aircraft? What might that be? There are no special troops in Gandamak. Nothing but tribesmen who have no love for the British."

Smithers chimes in, "What the bloody hell is a radio?"

It is clear to Sergeant Bishop that things are different from what he might have thought when approaching the hill. This group of soldiers is as bad off as he has ever seen. Many are in no more than rags of their former uniforms. Once fancy headgear is crushed under a cloth wrapped around the head and ears. It's a wonder how they've survived so far.

He looks at the confusion he has caused by using words that they do not understand. How will he explain?

# Chapter Three: Getting to Know Each Other

Lieutenant Short leaves his soldiers, looks at Lieutenant Wilkinson closely, and exclaims, "Lieutenant, when did you arrive in the country, and where are you based?"

Wilkinson stands stiffly and replies, "Leftenant, our regiment is the 44th East Sussex Regiment, established in 1714 with a proud history of defending the crown for the past one hundred fifty years. Our orders are to join the garrison at Jalalabad. We started the march five days ago after General Sir William Elphinstone arranged a truce."

"Lieutenant, I am a bit confused," says Short. "When did you leave Kabul?"

"We left on the 8th of January."

"Wilkinson, that's not possible. I was in Kabul on the 8th, and no British forces were there."

"Leftenant Short, I can assure you that the regiment was indeed in Kabul and had been there for three years. We arrived in 1839 from England."

"Wait just a minute, Wilkinson. Did you arrive in 1839? That's a hundred and eighty-four years ago!"

"I beg your pardon, Leftenant. The year is 1842. What are you talking about?"

"Wilkinson, let me try to figure out what happened because there is a great deal I don't understand. For me and my soldiers, it is the year 2023. We were flying to Kandahar when our aircraft crashed. We lost five members of the platoon and the flight crew. We are trying to reach the Special Forces camp at Gandamak to arrange a rescue."

"Leftenant Short, I am afraid you are badly mistaken. The year is 1842, and we have lost almost the entire regiment on the march to Jalalabad. Furthermore, we know of no camp of any kind at Gandamak. There is no chance of rescue for either of us. Our continued survival depends upon reaching Jalalabad."

Short, clearly bewildered, and at a loss for words, turns to Wilkinson and says, "I need to figure out what is going on. Let me get with my soldiers and decide what, if anything, we can do. " He then heads to where his soldiers are gathered on the hill's south side.

Wilkinson nods his acknowledgment, and as Short departs, he turns to Sergeant Smyth. "Color Sergeant, what do you think of our new arrivals?"

"Leftenant, I surely don't know what to think. They have these puny little rifles and carry all sorts of kit I have never seen. I wonder if they can help us in any way. We are better off with more soldiers, but what they can do is a mystery. All of their lads are a head or more taller than our lads. Maybe they are from a different line of the Army?"

While Lieutenants Short and Wilkinson were talking, Medic Sharon Kramer moved to one of the wagons, which was used as an ambulance. As she climbs into the wagon, she is surprised by the number of injuries each of the five soldiers has suffered. The bloodstained bandages do little to conceal the nature of their wounds, and the blackened fingers indicate severe frostbite. She is almost afraid to examine any feet. They will be worse, she is confident.

Her examination of an unconscious Captain Souter indicates he has a wound in his abdomen. After peeling back his bandages, she concludes that the wound has turned septic. And the other four wounded are in poor shape from exposure and their wounds. Opening her combat medic bag, she finds her most potent antibiotic and injects it into Captain Souter's shoulder. She realizes that her options are limited and that Captain Souter is not likely to survive.

The other wounded watch with wide eyes as Kramer attends to Captain Souter. She has removed her Kevlar helmet, and the ponytail of hair usually tucked in the back of her helmet has fallen loose. One of the wounded soldiers looks at her in surprise and exclaims, "A woman nurse! I never expected to see one in this godforsaken land. The good Lord must be looking after us after all."

Specialist Kramer smiles and responds, "Lucky for you, soldier. I have some medicine that will help you and your friends."

The next thirty minutes are spent giving oral antibiotic medicine to each of the wounded soldiers, applying antibiotic dressings, and rebandaging their wounds with the appropriate field dressings.

Slightly delirious, Private Paxton looks at Kramer and softly asks, "Will you marry me? You are the most beautiful woman I have ever seen."

Before she can respond, Private Maggard rises from his litter and rebukes Paxton: "You twit, she is a soldier and a doctor! She'll have nothing to do with an idiot such as you!"

A little bemused, Kramer looks at the four conscious but wounded and frostbitten soldiers and thinks, "What can I say to these tough men? My limited ability to treat their wounds and their frostbite will sustain them for a few days. After that, what will happen to them?"

Before she can organize her thoughts, a clearly older member of the unit says, "Now, you men, this doctor is something we have never seen before. She is treating us better than our surgeon has ever done. Be thankful that we have received our care from her."

Kramer turns to the speaker, "Thank you, soldier. I will continue to do my best to assist you in your recovery. Please be mindful of the dressings I have applied. They should protect your wounds for the next day." With that, Specialist Kramer climbs down from the wagon and slumps down on the snow-covered ground.

"This is so much harder than I ever imagined," she thinks as tears form in her eyes. "What more can I do?"

Before LT Short can organize his thoughts for the discussion with every member of the platoon, Doc Kramer approaches and says,

"LT, these guys are in terrible shape. Every one of them is wounded and frostbitten. Captain Souter will not make it another twenty-four hours without immediate evacuation. If we could, everyone in this outfit would need some medical treatment. I can only do so much."

"Doc, I know you will do all you can. But any medical evacuation is unlikely to happen anytime soon. If you can, look at the other soldiers in the unit and see what you can do to help them."

"Roger, sir. I suspect the best we can offer now is food and warmth. If we each provided one of our hot packs and an MRE, it would help offset some of the frostbite and the nutritional deficiencies they are suffering from. If I remember, we salvaged a couple of cold-weather survival kits from the Chinook. They have the emergency blankets to help the wounded in the wagons."

"Sharon, after I meet with the entire platoon, get with Sergeant Jackson and see how we can better utilize what we have. I trust your judgment on how best to help the British soldiers."

"No sweat, sir. I'll give it my best."

# Chapter Four: Assessing the Situation

Lieutenant Short turns to Sergeant Jackson, "Wil, I want every platoon member to know the situation is not what we thought it was. I must let everyone know what I think has happened and what we see going on right now."

Platoon Sergeant Jackson gathers the group of soldiers. They huddle around LT Short as he speaks.

"This is confusing to all of us, so let me outline what I think is happening. First, it appears that we somehow ended up back in 1842. Second, this British unit has traveled from Kabul, intending to reach its garrison at Jalalabad. They have lost almost an entire regiment along the way and have been given an ultimatum by the leader of the group attacking them. The ultimatum is surrender or be wiped out. Since we have appeared and joined with the British unit, the bad guys assume we are part of them. Simply put, we either surrender or fight. How we get back to 2023 and our families is unknown. What is known is that if we lose this fight, there will be no going home."

"Questions? Yes, SGT Bishop."

Sir, what the hell? How can a helo crash throw us back a hundred years?"

"Bishop, I have no clue how this happened, but the changes in the terrain and the fact that we can't get any comms seem to confirm that we are not where and when we thought we were. The presence of this British unit and its condition confirm what the British officer told me.

If, as he says, we are in 1842, our chances of being rescued by our guys are zero. However, if we can survive this fight, we can figure out how to return to our place and time. Our priority right now is to figure out how we can survive this fight."

"SGT Jackson, how are we fixed for weapons and ammo?"

"LT, both 249s are operational with about 800 rounds each. We don't have any sixties. The 60 mm mortar is ready to go; among the twenty-five of us, we are carrying 50 rounds. Each squad has two 320s, and each grenadier has about twenty rounds. Each M4 is operational, and we have lots of 5.56 we salvaged from the aircraft."

Short breathes a short sigh of relief and turns to the group. "Guys, if we are in 1842 and the bad guys are shooting at us with muskets, I think we have a distinct firepower advantage, regardless of how many there are. SGT Jackson and I will get with the British leadership and see how we can help them and us survive this fight. Meanwhile, break out your winter survival gear, get a fire going, and get some chow."

Short and Jackson move to where Lieutenant Wilkinson and SGT Smyth are huddled around a small fire. They look around at the other soldiers in the British unit and wonder how they have managed to survive. Their uniforms are in rags. Blankets are wrapped around their necks and heads, and bandaged hands grip Brown Bess muskets.

"Lieutenant Wilkinson, my soldiers and I are prepared and willing to do whatever is necessary to support your move to Jalalabad. May I suggest that before you move from this hill, we provide you and the groups attacking you with an example of the firepower we bring to this fight?"

"Leftenant Short, what do you have in mind?"

"If you will walk with me around the perimeter of the hill so that SGT Jackson and I can get some idea of what we are facing, I can plan our action more effectively?"

"Leftenant, I would like nothing better."

The two officers and two sergeants spend the next hour walking the perimeter of the hill. Along the way, Lieutenant Wilkinson addresses the soldiers by name and often offers reassurance and encouragement. Lieutenant Short is repeatedly surprised by the poor physical condition of the British soldiers. He is also warmly greeted by many who look quizzically at his uniform and weapons. He thinks to himself, "If this is all that is left of a 1200-member regiment, these guys have been through hell."

Meanwhile, SGT Jackson and SGT Smyth identified turbaned fighters gathered in small groups about 500 meters away. None appears to be ready to attack, although an occasional musket ball lands at the base of the hill. SGT Jackson turns to SGT Smyth and asks, "Sergeant, how many weapons do you have and how much ammunition?"

Smyth replies, "We have but twenty operating muskets and two cartridges each."

Jackson tries hard to keep the look of surprise off his face and asks, "What is the plan if you are attacked?"

With a disdainful smirk, Smyth replies, "We will use the bayonet, of course."

Jackson smiles and replies, "I hope we can keep that as the last resort."

Short and Wilkinson return to the fire being tended by one of the British privates and contemplate what may be next. Wilkinson knows little of what Short and his soldiers can do. Short, however, sees many possibilities for negating the numerical advantage the attackers appear to have.

While waiting for the two sergeants to return, Short looks at Wilkinson and asks, "Lieutenant, how long have you been in Afghanistan?"

Wilkinson grimaces and replies, "The regiment arrived in 1839. I joined the regiment after finishing school in 1833. And you, Leftenant, how long have you been in this godforsaken country?"

"My unit and I arrived a year ago. This is SGT Jackson's second time in Afghanistan, but the rest of us have never been here before."

"How did you come to find us and join in this ill-fated journey? Your weapons and kit are so very different than any I have ever seen. Where are you from, and how did you get to where we are now?"

Lieutenant Wilkinson, you are going to find this hard to believe, but we were enroute to Kandahar when our helicopter crashed about five miles from here. A number of my unit's members were killed in the crash, and we had no way of contacting anyone who could come to our assistance. It is January 2023 for us, and I have no idea how we came to be with you in 1842."

"Leftenant, how can that be? I surmise from your speech and the markings on your uniforms and weapons that you are from America, but how did an American army unit arrive in time to help us in 1842?"

Before either lieutenant could continue the conversation, both sergeants arrived with a rough concept of the forces facing them. SGT Jackson begins with, "I counted multiple groups of from thirty to fifty armed with rifles. Most are also carrying some sort of sword. There is no evidence of crew-served weapons or direct or indirect fire. All the groups are currently within range of all of our weapons. They appear to be regrouping and preparing for an attack."

LT Short turns to Wilkinson, "Lieutenant, I will have SGT Jackson deploy our soldiers along the upper slope of the hill. I suggest your soldiers move to the lower slope, as our weapons will be firing over them. You may want to have your soldiers hold their limited ammunition for later, as we have enough for our weapons to deter any attackers."

Wilkinson turns to Smyth, "SGT Smyth, let us take advantage of Leftenant Short's offers and move our soldiers to the lower slope as soon as possible."

As the Americans deploy around the crest of the hill, Wilkinson and Smyth have difficulty understanding what the individual soldiers are doing. Accustomed to the employment of muskets in multiple ranks of soldiers, the placement of individual soldiers in prone and covered positions is a significant difference they have never seen.

The strange square packages attached to each little rifle are another strange piece of equipment they have never seen.

# Chapter Five: The First Fight

SGT Jackson and Lieutenant Short move around their soldiers, now positioned on the upper slope of the hill. As they walk, SGT Jackson says, "LT, the ragheads have no idea what hell we can rain down on them. They expect to be facing the same muskets the Brits have been using for the past few days. I suggest we let them get within two hundred meters and then have a mad minute with the 249s and the M4s. Once they pull back, we can finish with some 40mikemike from the 320s."

"Sounds like a plan. Let's make sure each machine gunner keeps it to fifty rounds and the 320s to three grenades each. M4s no more than two magazines. As Short and Jackson ensure each of their soldiers understands the plan, groups of mufti-clothed figures begin to move to the hill from the north and east. Some groups number as many as fifty, others less, but all are now waving both muskets and swords as they advance.

Most attackers are now firing wildly and stopping to reload. The groups approach more confidently as no return fire is received from the hill. As Short estimates the attackers are within 200 meters, he gives a loud "Fire!"

Two machine guns pour 5.56 rounds into the tightly packed groups, and 40-millimeter grenades explode among the following clusters. LT Short has two sharpshooters with long-range 7.62 rifles targeting any attackers who appear to be leaders. One by one, any robed figure trying to reorganize or direct others is hit by the precise long-range fire.

The blast of unexpected fire stops the two attacking groups in seconds and piles up bodies by the dozens. The snow is stained red for fifty feet around the many bodies. Well-aimed single shots from the Americans pick off individual attackers attempting to retreat. LT Short finally calls a cease-fire as a few walking wounded struggle to move away from the stacked bodies.

The British soldiers rise from their seated positions on the lower portion of the hill and look at the Americans with a mix of expressions. Most appear awestruck, while others seek to understand what they have just seen. They turn to each other as if there is some answer, for no British soldier has fired a shot.

SGT Smyth runs to LT Wilkinson and says, "Jasus Christ, Leftenant, what in God's name just happened? Do these fellas have some lightning they can unleash at will? I have never seen or heard anything like this in my life."

"Smyth, I have nothing to say. This is beyond my understanding. No weapons I know of can do what we just witnessed. We shall ask Leftenant Short to explain to us what we just witnessed."

The bodies that now lie motionless in the snow are approached by figures waving small white flags. It is soon apparent that these are burial parties. American and British soldiers watch stoically as the dead and wounded are carried from the now-bloody snowfield. While no one provides any estimate of the casualties, it is apparent that the tribesmen have suffered severe losses.

Short and Jackson, after checking their soldiers, join Wilkinson and Smyth. Short raises his hand and says, "Gentlemen, I know this has been a surprise, but when we arrived, there wasn't time to introduce our weapons to you and explain how we use them. With SGT Jackson's help, let me explain. SGT Jackson is carrying one of our rifles. It is also fitted with a grenade launcher and a scope that allows our soldiers to fire effectively out to 600 yards. Our rifles fire the bullet I have in my hand. The long, curved case in my other hand holds 30 of these bullets. A rifleman can select a single fire or a three-round burst. Although this bullet is much smaller than your musket balls, it travels much faster and farther and causes significant damage when it penetrates. The short tube under the muzzle of the rifle is a grenade launcher. The grenade SGT Jackson is holding is capable of traveling almost 600 yards, and when it lands and explodes, it will kill anything within five feet. A well-trained grenadier can drop one in your pocket at 200 yards. The rapid-fire sound you heard was our two machine guns. They also fire this same bullet but have a rate of fire of about 400 rounds a minute. That is what devastated the attackers, who were bunched up, expecting to be confronted with musket fire. I think we have given the group that demanded your surrender a serious setback. I also suspect they will hesitate to test us again in the same way."

Smyth looks at SGT Jackson and shakes his head, "Jackson, how long have you had these weapons?

Jackson smiles and replies, "Almost ten years, SGT Smyth. Each has had some improvements over the years, but they are essentially the same ones I had when I joined the Army twelve years ago."

"How can these be?" says Smyth. "Have you found some magic?"

"SGT Smyth, it's not magic but simply improvements in propellant and projectiles of a century in the making."

"Aye, so what you are telling me is that you and your men are from a different century? If that is so, you surely know what happened to the regiment in its march from Kabul."

"I can't say I can, SGT Smyth, as my knowledge of the history of English operations in Afghanistan is quite limited. I can tell you that we have been in the northern part for the past year and experienced some difficult fighting with the Taliban. Lieutenant Short may have more knowledge than I."

Both Wilkinson and Smyth turn to Lieutenant Short with obvious questions on their minds. Wilkinson asks first, "Leftenant, just where and when are you from?"

"Lieutenant Wilkinson and Sergeant Smyth, we left our headquarters outside Kabul two days ago aboard a United States Army helicopter. We encountered some severe weather over the mountains, and the aircraft crashed. We lost a portion of the platoon in the crash.

We were unable to communicate with our radios and have been attempting to reach the Special Forces camp in Gandamak to use their radios to call for pickup and return to our departure airfield in Kandahar. For us, today is January 13, 2023, or 181 years from now."

"Leftenant," says Smyth, "you have just used words I don't know. What is a helicopter, a radio, and who are special forces?

"Both are developments, and some might say inventions that will be made in the next fifty to eighty years. We refer to those soldiers with special training and experience as Special Forces. A helicopter is a machine that can take off from the ground and carry men and equipment long distances. A radio is another machine that can send our voices over long distances and allows us to coordinate our activities with Army units some distance from us. Neither of these will be available for another hundred years."

Wilkinson, now both confused and disconcerted by what he has just heard, forcefully interrupts, "Gentlemen, while the history lessons are appreciated, we need to consider how to extricate ourselves from the constant assaults and make our way to Jalalabad."

"Lieutenant Wilkinson, may Sergeant Jackson and I have some time to assess how we might best assist you? I assure you, we have some capabilities that could make your march easier."

"I appreciate that, Leftenant, and look forward to getting on the move as soon as we can. While most of the men remain unwounded, they are in poor physical condition. The terrain and the weather have taken a terrible toll on their bodies. I also have concerns for Captain Souter's survival."

Lieutenant Short calls Specialist Kramer, the platoon medic, to the leadership group and asks, "Doc, what's the status of the wounded and sick?"

"Sir, Captain Souter's wound is septic, and I don't think the antibiotics I gave him will make any difference. Without a medevac to a hospital, he isn't going to make it. The other three wounded are responding to the meds I have given them. I can do nothing for the frostbite that almost all the soldiers are experiencing. The longer they sit on this hilltop, the more frostbite they will have."

It is now Smyth's turn to ask an obvious question, "Do you have a woman doctor in your formation? I have seen her minister to the soldiers, but did not realize she was a woman. Can she provide the medical support needed?"

Jackson smiles, "SGT Smyth, Specialist Kramer is a trained combat medic. She can treat almost any injury or ailment in the field. Unfortunately, there is little she can do to treat frostbite, which is a significant concern.

"LT Short, I recommend that, if possible, we get moving from here. Staying around much longer is going to prolong the suffering of many of these soldiers, and our guys aren't going to be doing any better much longer."

"I agree, Sergeant Jackson. Lieutenant Wilkinson, we shall support your move to Jalalabad."

"Leftenant Short, with your weapons, we may be able to establish our garrison. We had expected to make a final stand on this hill. May I suggest that we depart at first light in the morning, as it will be nightfall in just a few hours?"

"I agree, Wilkinson. We may be able to offer the attackers some more surprises. Sergeant Jackson, can we determine where the attacking groups are massing for the attacks or where they may be bedding down for the night?"

As the two walk away from the still-amazed British leadership, Platoon Sergeant Jackson says.

"Lieutenant, why don't we do a night recon and find out where these ragheads are? As Lieutenant Wilkinson said, it will be dark in a few hours. We still have a few working NODs, and a couple of us could really scope out the situation."

"Agree. Get with Wilson and Bishop and come up with a plan for no more than three to conduct a recon of the area where we think the ragheads may be congregating. I don't want anyone wandering around too long, but just ID what we need to know."

Platoon Sergeant Jackson walks to where SGT Wilson and SGT Bishop are talking with some of the British soldiers. He can't help but smile when one of the British soldiers says, "Aye, now, SGT Wilson, what country is your army from?" Before Wilson can answer, Jackson interrupts and asks both squad leaders to come with him. He grins at the British soldier who asked the question and says, "We are the United States Army. You know, the one that won the war with England in 1779?" The puzzled look on the British soldier's face made it clear to Jackson that the soldier had no idea what he was talking about. Meanwhile, Wilson and Bishop have moved to a spot where the three of them can talk.

Jackson opens the gathering with, "We need to do some recon before morning. The plan is to help this British unit make its way to its garrison in Jalalabad. From the looks of them and the number of ragheads attacking, they won't make it without us. The lieutenant wants a three-man patrol to look for the assembly areas or the night locations of the ragheads. If they are in range, we will drop some 60 mortar rounds on them and discourage any further attacks. Wilson, Bishop, this is a volunteer mission. I understand the stress that everyone is in, and no way I am going to force someone to be on the patrol."

Bishop says, "Top, I got it. I'll take Thompson and Jones. I know they will volunteer. We can go out after hard dark. Any ideas on the direction, or should we do a 360?"

"Thanks, Bishop. Round up three good working NODs, and you will carry one of the working squad radios. We want to keep in contact if we can. Wilson, you and Bishop get with your troops. I want to make sure everyone is watching their chow because God knows how long we will be here."

"Top, we figured we had about four days' rations. Water doesn't appear to be a problem. The Brits say there are a number of wells between here and their garrison. Honest to God, I have never seen a more beat-up bunch of soldiers. Most of these guys are down to two or three rounds for their muskets. It looks like none of them have ever heard of cold-weather gear."

"Let's share what we can spare, but I don't want our soldiers giving away things that they or we are going to need in the next couple of days."

Bishop, attempting to inject some humor, quips, "like M4s?"

"Yes, smart ass, like our M4s. For God's sake, don't let any of the Brits handle our weapons or hand grenades. We can't afford any friendly fire. Bishop, as soon as you can get the gear together, we will get with the Lieutenant and work out your patrol."

"Roger Top, we should be ready right after we get something to eat. Say, about an hour."

Platoon Sergeant Jackson looks for Lieutenant Short, sees him talking intently with Lieutenant Wilkinson, and decides to give them more uninterrupted time together.

The conversation between Short and Wilkinson is strange because Wilkinson first asks Short, "Are you really from the future? If so, do you know how England fares in Afghanistan?"

"Wilkinson, all I can recall is that the British Army withdrew from the country after a series of military defeats. If one of those is the situation we are in right now, I don't know. I do know there will be a second occupation by the British Army, but my history is fuzzy on that outcome."

"Short, what can you tell me about your country and how you came to be in Afghanistan? Surely, things have changed in the past 180 years."

"Strangely enough, I don't think things have changed that much. In my time, Afghanistan is still run much along the tribal and ethnic allegiances it is in your time. What has changed is the weapons and the people who use them. For example, we have lost more soldiers to IEDs, which are improvised explosive devices, than to actual gunfire. Technological improvements work both ways in combat. We may be able to do many things you cannot in this day and age, but so too does the native fighter do things that he could not a hundred years ago.

SGT Bishop, Specialist Thompson, and PFC Jones share some of their MREs with three British soldiers. One of the British soldiers comments, "How does your food in a bag stay so warm? I dinna see you heat it over the fire."

SGT Bishop, motioning with his plastic fork, replies, "We have a chemical mixture in the bottom that heats up quickly and provides a warm meal. What do you think of it?"

Paxton, the British private, shakes his head, "I dinna know what was in what is called chili con carne, but it was hot and filled me. Can you, lads, pull more out of that box? It's the most food I have had in many days."

"Let's go easy on the chow. We have a couple more days before we get more."

"Paxton, how long have you been in the Army?"

Private Paxton considers the question and replies simply, "Forever, it seems. I joined the regiment when I turned sixteen. We have been to the West Indies, Mesopotamia, and now Iraq. I haven't seen my family in Wessex since '38 when the regiment was shipped to this godforsaken country. We lost most of the lads on our march from Kabul. These tribesmen are fierce demons. They haven't given us a moment's rest for the last five days."

# Chapter Six: Night Action and Move-Out

SGT Bishop, Specialist Thompson, and PFC Jones put on their camouflage paint, adjust their NODs (night observation devices), and review Lieutenant Short's map. Bishop tells the Lieutenant, "We will move west for about a klick, then turn south for about two klicks, and then head back around to the east and north. I'll mark on the map where we find any ragheads."

Short acknowledges and adds, "That sounds good, Scott. Sergeant Jackson and I will have the other two squad radios, so give us a sitrep every five minutes. If I don't hear from you in ten minutes, we will head to your last location."

"Roger, sir. I'll rely on Thompson to remind me to make the sitreps.

At 0100, the three members of the recon team move west from the hill. Almost immediately, their NODs pick up firelight due west and southwest. Traveling slowly and watching for any sign of tribesmen, the three place a marker on the map where the first and largest fire is located. They can see a group of figures huddled around the fire but are unable to determine how many may be scattered around smaller fires in the distance. For the next two hours, the three have identified five separate locations where the largest groups of tribesmen have bedded down for the night. The number of fires at each location is different, and the number of individual fighters cannot be determined. Tired and cold, the three soldiers return to the hill to find

Lieutenant Short and Platoon Sergeant Jackson waiting for them with hot coffee. After Sergeant Bishop, Sergeant Jackson and Lieutenant Short go over the map, Lieutenant Short says,

"Well done, SGT Bishop." I see five prime locations for some night mortar action. Can we get a good estimate on the range to each location?"

"Yes, sir. If we shoot an azimuth to each location marked on the map, figuring out the range should be easy. Garcia is a trained mortarman; he can easily hit those spots with two rounds."

Sergeant Jackson is already on his way to Garcia's location and tells him to bring up the 60 mortar and round up ten rounds. Specialist Garcia joins the group and sets up the 60mm mortar bipod. After reviewing the locations on the map and shooting an azimuth to each one, he turns to the group and says, "All of these locations are well within range. SGT Bishop, how close are the markings to the center of the groups?"

"Garcia, I think we got each one of them within five or ten yards."

Garcia turns to Lieutenant Short, "Sir, I think we can get two rounds into each of these locations in less than ten minutes. I won't need to do many adjustments in range, mostly just in deflection."

"Garcia, you may begin planning on dropping two rounds on each location. I suggest you start with the ones closest and hit the farther ones last."

"Got it, sir. Me and Specialist Murtaugh will start making the adjustments."

Garcia and Murtaugh begin calculating the mortar's range and deflection and lay out the mortar rounds with the appropriate charges for each target. Within ten minutes, Garcia asks, "Lieutenant, we are ready to start firing. Do we want to alert everyone on the hill or let it be a surprise to them, as well?"

Lieutenant Short turns to the mortar crew and tells Specialist Garcia, "Our guys know what a mortar sounds like, so I'm not concerned about their reaction. I'll get with Lieutenant Wilkinson and let him know what we are doing."

Lieutenant Short and Sergeant Jackson move to the small fire that Lieutenant Wilkinson and Sergeant Smyth were sharing.

"Sergeant Smyth, where may I find Lieutenant Wilkinson?"

"I believe he went with your doctor to check on Captain Souter."

Short moves quickly to where the two wagons are parked and asks one of the soldiers tending the fire if Lieutenant Wilkinson is around.

"Aye, sir. The Leftenant is attending to the Captain in the first wagon. Shall I tell him you are here?"

Lieutenant Wilkinson joins Lieutenant Short within minutes. Short immediately notices that Wilkinson is more solemn than before and asks, "How is your Captain?"

"He didn't survive his wound," says Wilkinson. "I had my hopes that he would. I believe your doctor did all she could. What is so urgent this time of night?"

"I have more firepower to hit the tribesmen with and wanted to alert your soldiers that we are firing and for them to not be alarmed. The sounds they hear will be unfamiliar to them, but the explosions on the tribesmen will be heard for miles."

"I assume these are weapons you haven't told me about?"

"Actually, Wilkinson, the weapon is old; it was just updated, and the projectiles were modernized considerably. We will be firing a mortar at positions my soldiers identified during their reconnaissance tonight."

"Have your soldiers been wandering around at night looking for tribesmen? That doesn't seem prudent. Getting lost in the dark is hardly a good way to fight."

"Never fear. We have vision devices that allow us to see at night and operate in even the darkest of nights. Our recon party located five groups within range, and we shall be putting some hardware on them very shortly. I recommend you pass the word to your soldiers that we will be firing ten rounds in total. They may recognize the mortar firing, but the explosions on the tribesmen will be unmistakable.

"Lieutenant Wilkinson, after we drop the ordnance on the tribesmen, I think we should move out as soon as possible, maybe even starting before first light. If we can get moving before the ragheads reorganize, it will give us a break before they think about attacking again."

I suggest that we prepare to move as soon as possible. Our mortar attack should disrupt the tribesmen's plans and give us some respite from their attacks."

Wilkinson is taken aback and replies, "Are you and your soldiers ready to move and support our march to Jalalabad?"

"We are; the sooner we get there, the better."

As Lieutenant Short returns to his mortar crew, Lieutenant Wilkinson finds Sergeant Smyth. They pass the word around the hill that the Americans will be firing, and there is no cause for concern. He also instructs the senior corporals to prepare their soldiers for an immediate departure.

At approximately 0400 on a cold winter day, one by one, two 60mm mortar rounds descend on each of the five groups of tribesmen. At least one of the two rounds fired on each location hits the center of the tents grouped around small fires. The resulting explosions delight all the British soldiers on the hill as they begin to see that their situation is not as hopeless as it once was. With renewed energy, the British soldiers acknowledge the orders of their corporals and begin collecting what meager belongings they have salvaged on the march.

Short and Wilkinson call Sergeant Jackson and Sergeant Smyth to the dying embers of their fire and address the route of march.

Short begins, "Sergeant Jackson, if some of the British need help, we need to identify them as soon as possible. The two wagons look in good shape, but the horses are on their last legs." I want the first squad, SGT Wilson, to be our lead security element. They will have one of the working squad radios and stay about a klick ahead of the column. The second squad, SGT Bishop, will be the trail security and have the second squad radio. I will keep the third radio, and you and I can monitor both lead and trail elements. I want Specialist Garcia and the automatic weapons in the center of the march. They are the response to any attacks from the north or south. Any questions?"

Lieutenant Wilkinson asks, "Leftenant Short, how do we best respond to any attacks on our column? As you may know, we can travel only as fast as the wagons will allow."

"Lieutenant Wilkinson, if all goes as planned, there will be no surprise attacks, and I think our firepower will keep most of the tribesmen at a distance. I suggest we move immediately once all the wounded are loaded in the wagons."

"Leftenant, fear not, the 44th Foot will be ready to move on command," says Sergeant Smyth.

As a false dawn pales the dark winter sky, Lieutenant Short does a commo check with his two squad leaders, receives confirmation that they are ready, and orders SGT Wilson to move out.

SGT Wilson turns to his designated point man, Specialist Waters. "Waters, now is the time for you to move. Keep a lookout for any of the ragheads, and use your arm and hand signals to alert us. This is a free-fire zone, so if you happen upon any ragheads that appear hostile, take them out. I suggest that you keep one of the M320s available if you need to hit a group."

"I gotcha, Sergeant Wilson. The sooner we get away from this god-forsaken place and out of the cold, the better."

# Chapter Seven: The Journey Begins

The British soldiers line up in a column of twos, half in front and half following the two wagon loads of wounded. Specialist Garcia and the two machine gunners fall in on each side of the two wagons. The two designated sharpshooters are positioned along the front half of the column and the back half of the column. Lieutenant Short and Lieutenant Wilkinson are leading the column of twos while SGT Wilson has his squad within sight and covering the entire front of the march.

Lieutenant Short turns to Lieutenant Wilkinson, "How far do you think we are from Jalalabad? Do you have a map that we can review? If not, we should look at mine and try to determine the distance."

The two lieutenants step away from the line of troops and look at Short's map.

"Wilkinson, I estimate between eight and ten miles, but that is a straight-line distance. I am unfamiliar with the track between here and Jalalabad, so it could add another two to three miles."

"I agree, Short. We are moving so slowly; I have doubts we can reach Jalalabad before dark tomorrow."

SGT Wilson calls back to Lieutenant Short, "We are having trouble following the trail. Has anyone in the British unit been on this trail before? With the snow cover, I am not sure we are on the right trail."

"Hang on, SGT Wilson. Let me check," says Lieutenant Short as he turns to Lieutenant Wilkinson. "Has anyone from your regiment traveled this road before? My soldiers are having a difficult time following the road with the snow cover."

"Sergeant Smyth," yells Lieutenant Wilkinson, "Who has traveled this road before? Anyone?"

"Leftenant, I be the only one left who has traveled the road from Kabul to Kandahar."

"Sergeant Smyth, please join Sergeant Wilson ahead and assist in keeping on the road. We best not wander."

"Aye, sir, and a hard road it is for the next five miles. There be two places between here and Kandahar where the tribesmen will want to ambush us. If I may, Leftenant Short, I can mark those on your map and take them to Sergeant Wilson."

"Please do, Sergeant Smyth. SGT Wilson also has a map, but you can exchange mine with your markings."

With map in hand, Smyth joins SGT Wilson about 200 meters ahead of the column.

"SGT Wilson, I have traveled this road before and will endeavor to help us stay on the road to Jalalabad. I also need to show you some locations ahead that may be troublesome. I have Lieutenant Short's map and have marked the locations I believe the tribesmen can best use to attack us."

"Thanks, Sergeant Smyth. Following this road with the snow cover from the last few days is becoming harder and harder. Let's move over to the rocks and check the map."

The two sergeants go over the map and the locations Smyth suggests would be possible attack sites for the tribesmen. As Wilson refolds his map, a musket ball lands twenty feet behind them. Specialist Costanza calls out, "Ragheads firing on us at 10 o'clock. We are engaging with grenades and 5.56."

Costanza launches a 40mm grenade at the location he saw two figures firing from. As the grenade explodes, two figures run from their covered position and attempt to retreat. Costanza and Waters fire and the two figures drop. A silence follows the rapid gunfire.

Sergeant Wilson and Sergeant Smyth point toward a break in the terrain. Wilson calls to Waters, "Head toward that break in the terrain at your one o'clock. That's the road."

Waters moves toward the break in the terrain and turns to Sergeant Wilson, "Ron, I got a bad feeling about this. Can we put a couple of 40 mikemikes on the sides?"

"Roger, Tim. One on each side."

Lieutenant Short and Wilkinson watch the explosions on either side of the cut through the terrain. Almost before the dust cloud from the explosions has cleared, small groups of tribesmen hurry east.

"Leftenant Short, I believe your weapons send a strong message to the tribesmen that they are not to delay our progress to Jalalabad."

"It could be a long day. Let's hope the ragheads are as uncoordinated as they appear," says Short.

"Where does that term you use, ragheads come from?"

Short replies, "I don't really know. When the United States was attacked on 9/11, we learned the planning and support came from Afghanistan. Since then, anyone wearing a headscarf in Afghanistan is called a raghead."

"9/11, what is that? Who attacked America?

"It's a long story, Wilkinson. If and when we get to Jalalabad, I will fill you in. Meanwhile, I need to get up with the lead element and see if there are any problems."

Short joins Sergeants Wilson and Smyth as they watch Waters and Costanza climb the rocks that concealed the tribesmen. Waters climbs down and joins Wilson, Smyth, and Short.

"Lieutenant, it looks to me like the two we took down running away were here for a while. There is a third raghead behind the rocks that took the full blast from the 40mikemike. There was bedding and cooking pots and a fire pit. I would guess at least a couple of days."

Lieutenant Short turns to Sergeant Smyth, "Sergeant Smyth, what do you make of what was found?"

"Leftenant, I am not sure. These tribesmen are a crafty lot. They may well have a small bunch watching our every move. As long as they keep their distance, their presence doesn't seem a problem."

"How did they attack you on the road from Kabul? Can we learn anything from those attacks?"

"Leftenant, to be truthful, the tribesmen simply came at us in force. Once within range of their muskets, they fired volley after volley. We made a good account of ourselves, but for every five our lads shot, we lost one of our own. The five days on the road from Kabul was one long firing line."

As he turns to leave, Lieutenant Short says, "Sergeant Smyth, if the tribesmen have learned anything from our recent engagements, assembling a large force may not work out as they expect.

# Chapter Eight: The Challenge is Clear

The morning sky is clear and cold. The British soldiers move slowly. Lieutenant Short notices that more than half the American soldiers are now carrying bags that were once on the shoulders of a British soldier.

Lieutenant Wilkinson walks alongside Lieutenant Short and remarks, "Leftenant, this is a difficult slog. I think we need to give the lads a break, get some warming fires going, and get some hot tea in as many as possible."

"I agree," says Short, "but let my soldiers establish a perimeter out 200 yards and give all your sentries a chance to warm up and eat something."

"That would be splendid, and while we have little food to offer, could you take the time to eat with me?"

"I would like to do that, and I hope you feel comfortable using my first name, which is Roger. I also have a surprise for you. We have rations that I can heat up quickly, and I think you will enjoy."

Lieutenant Wilkinson quickly responds, "Roger, that would be lovely. And, please, my name is James. Do your rations from the future provide more sustenance than those in my time?

"I will let you be the judge of that, James."

Lieutenant Short reflects on the speech patterns demonstrated by Wilkinson. Although he has had little contact with British officers, it is clear to him that James is from an aristocratic family, and his background is far different from those of his soldiers.

Platoon Sergeant Jackson contacts Sergeants Wilson and Bishop, instructing them to establish the perimeter. Wilson's squad is from 12 o'clock to 6 o'clock, and Bishop's squad is from 6 o'clock to 12 o'clock.[1] As the perimeter is being established, Sergeant Smyth and the senior corporals are breaking out what little firewood is available and making small warming fires. A few volunteer cooks begin making hot water and are soon distributing hot tea to the bedraggled British soldiers.

The two lieutenants scrape away snow from the two large rocks they have selected around a small fire. Short digs around in his rucksack, pulls out two dark green bags, and turns to Wilkinson.

"James, I can offer you one of two meals: meatballs in marinara sauce or beef stew. I am happy with either one. Before you make your selection, I must tell you that the meatball dinner comes with a cherry blueberry cobbler while the beef stew has a pound cake."

"My God, Roger. Where and how do you find these in that bag? I must go for the beef stew, but how will you heat such a meal?"

"James, our food scientists have developed a bag that contains chemicals that, once combined, produce heat. I place the bag of the

---

[1] 12 o'clock is always the direction of march. 6 o'clock is the tail of the formation.

beef stew in the bag with the chemicals, and within minutes, the meal is heated. I must warn you that it will be quite hot initially."

Lieutenant Wilkinson looks on as Lieutenant Short prepares both meals and heats the accompanying drinks and condiments. He repeatedly exclaims while savoring his beef stew,

"What jolly good food. It is no wonder your lads are a head taller and broader than the British soldier. With rations like these, we could not be defeated. I haven't had a meal like this since my last meal in the Regimental Mess."

"I remember you said you joined your regiment in 1836," said Short. "Where was the regiment, and how did you join it?"

"The regiment is based in West Essex in the southeast of England and was raised by my great-grandfather in 1744. My grandfather served in the regiment for only ten years when he died in the war with France in 1782. My father joined the regiment in 1800 as a subaltern and eventually left in 1835 as lieutenant colonel. As the Earl of Sussex, he remained a patron of the regiment. You could almost say that the regiment is a part of my family for at least three generations."

Short finishes his meal and asks Wilkinson, "I am not sure what you mean. So, what is an Earl?"

Wilkinson replies. "The title is given by the monarch and passed from the father to the firstborn son. My family has had land in the County of Sussex since the 1300s. The title was awarded for service to the crown and is the second-highest rank in nobility in England.

As if to punctuate his statement, rifle fire from the north of the column gives notice that the rest of the journey will be contested. Lieutenant Short calls Sergeants Wilson and Bishop for an update. Bishop replies, "We spotted a couple of ragheads setting up about 400 meters from us in covered positions. Our fire made them quit their positions and run to the east. No more ragheads observed."

"James, it appears we are encouraged to continue our hike to Jalalabad. Let me secure our meals, and I will have our lead elements move forward to find any more likely ambush locations."

Once the column starts moving east, Sergeant Wilson and Sergeant Smyth review the map and see the first possible ambush site a kilometer ahead. Wilson directs Specialist Waters and Costanza to move out and put grenades on the terrain feature.

"Costanza, how many grenades do you have?"

"Waters, I have a dozen. One or two at each possible hide location should flush out any bad guys."

"Let's move, I'll cover you.

Waters and Costanza are within 400 meters of the possible ambush site and stop for Costanza to load his M320 grenade launcher. As soon as Costanza drops the first round on a possible hide site, a half dozen tribesmen rise up from a second hide site and fire a volley at the two American soldiers. Caught in the open, both soldiers hit the ground and return fire. Before the six tribesmen can reload their muskets, accurate M4 fire drops all six. Costanza immediately fires another grenade and hits the second identified hide site, and then another grenade on the now prone and wounded six who were attempting to ambush the column.

"Whew, shit Costanza. We would be dead meat if these guys didn't have to reload."

"What the hell, Waters? Haven't these guys got the message? Muskets against M4s and 320s are a losing proposition. Let me give the LT an update. They would have heard the firing."

Waters waits for Sergeant Wilson to join them and gives Lieutenant Short an update on the squad radio.

Continuing to lead the column, Lieutenant Short turns to Lieutenant Wilkinson and says, "James, as we thought, the tribesmen are looking to engage the column wherever possible. The lead element just eliminated six of them at the first danger point identified by Sergeant Smyth."

"Roger, how far are we from the next danger point? I think we may want to have another stop before reaching that location. Many of our soldiers are much the worse for wear."

"I believe we have made about two and a half miles. The next danger point is about a mile away. I suggest we make another half mile and then have a rest and warming stop."

"Let us make that location as soon as possible."

# Chapter Nine: A Difficult Decision

For the past three hours, 3rd platoon members have been sharing both food and warm clothing with their British counterparts. Despite their efforts, a few British soldiers are unable to maintain the pace and fall from fatigue and malnourishment. American soldiers are quick to pick them up and provide support. Lieutenant Wilkinson realizes that it may be futile to continue at this pace. Lieutenant Short also recognizes that their pace is no longer possible and turns to Wilkinson, "James, how about we call it a day and see if we can't help some of your soldiers get strong enough to continue tomorrow?"

"Roger, my thoughts, exactly. We have left too many behind in days past. Let us not leave any almost within reach of our goal."

Many warming fires are lit, and American soldiers encourage their British counterparts to stay close to the fires as they break out more warm clothing from their rucksacks. Lieutenant Short asks Specialist Kramer, the platoon medic, to sit with him at a small outcropping of rocks.

"Sharon, what do you recommend we do? These soldiers are in bad shape. Some much worse than others and we have only a limited amount of food and clothing we can spare?"

Kramer has obviously given this considerable thought and replies, "Lieutenant, we need to focus on getting the weakest among them hydrated, fed, and warmed. I can do nothing for the frostbitten feet and hands. Many will lose fingers and toes, but if we provide some major attention to the weakest, I believe we can get them strong enough to continue in the morning."

Sergeant Smyth has identified his soldiers in the poorest condition and begins working with Doc Kramer and Specialist Garcia to provide hot chocolate, a hot meal, and the emergency blankets salvaged from the downed helicopter.

Sergeant Jackson makes the round of the perimeter established by elements of Sergeant Bishop and Wilson's squads.

"Bishop, how are your guys holding up?"

"I gotta tell you, Platoon Sergeant, that this sucks big time. I got one or two guys that might have frostbite, so I have them around the fire warming up. This miserable country and this shitty weather is a bad combination. The good news is we have plenty of ammo, and all weapons systems are go."

Reaching Sergeant Wilson, Jackson asks, "Ron, what does your squad look like? You have had most of the action today. Any issues?

"Top, we are all cold as shit and hungry. My guys have given the Brits most of their MREs, and tonight might be their last meal in their rucks. Just when one of the guys starts to complain, all he has to do is look at one of the Brits and shut up. I don't know how these guys made it as far as they have."

Platoon Sergeant Jackson looks around at the now-integrated group of British soldiers in their tattered uniforms of red and blue, as well as the desert camouflage of his own platoon. The contrast is so dramatic that Jackson has to shake off the feeling that this is some nightmare. As night falls, he reminds both Wilson and Bishop to rotate their guys on sentry duty more often than usual.

Wilkinson and Short are seated close to a warming fire and quickly share Short's last MRE. Short looks long and hard at Wilkinson and says, "James, how long has it been since you have had any communication with the garrison at Jalalabad?"

"I believe Captain Souter received a message from Jalalabad garrison shortly before we left. I don't know what this was because I only received orders to prepare for movement to Jalalabad and join the garrison there."

"James, I would assume that the garrison at Jalalabad is expecting you, at least the regiment?"

"Roger, that would be my assumption, as well."

"James, these last couple of miles may be the most difficult for some members of your company. I suggest a small party depart immediately for the garrison and request assistance for the remainder of your party to make it to Jalalabad during the day."

"But, Roger, how will we move to Jalalabad at night? We cannot travel at night and would likely never make it."

"James, we know that Sergeant Smyth has traveled this road and is the best to lead that party tonight. If we were to equip Sergeant Smyth with the means of seeing at night and had two of my soldiers with the same night vision devices with him, I believe they could make good time and not be interfered with by any tribesmen."

"Roger, while I agree in principle, let's put it to Sergeant Smyth and see if he can accomplish that mission."

Sergeant Smyth soon joins the two lieutenants around their warming fire. His immediate reaction to the plan is positive: "Leftenants, I can make my way to Jalalabad in the dark, and having two of the Americans with me would be comforting."

"Sergeant Smyth, I have a bit of technology that will help. I will let Sergeant Jackson help you mount the night vision device, and then the two of you can go beyond the fires and see how much nighttime vision you will have."

Sergeant Jackson approaches the group with one of the working NODs and fits it snugly around Sergeant Smyth's head. "Sergeant Smyth, you will flip down the eyepiece resting on your forehead once we are beyond the firelight. On the right side of the eyepiece is a switch. With your finger, push the switch up, and the eyepieces will show you everything that was in darkness is now in black and white."

The two senior sergeants move away from the warming fires and join the American soldiers on the perimeter.

"Sergeant Smyth, we have gone far enough. What can you see in the darkness?"

"Jackson, I see nothing but black even with the small moonlight overhead."

"Drop the eyepieces over your eyes and turn the switch I told you on the right side of the eyepiece."

"My God!!" says Smyth, "what kind of magic is this?"

"No magic, Smyth. The eyepieces just magnify the available light and project it onto your eyes."

"But, Jackson, it's all black and white. There are no colors."

"We haven't reached that point in the technology. But can you see to navigate the road to Jalalabad?"

"Aye, with no trouble at all now that I can see in the dark. Can I have one of your wee rifles to carry?"

"We must be careful with these night vision devices and avoid looking at lights. Even firelight may cause them to blank out. We have additional rifles. I will have one of our riflemen give you a quick tutorial on the weapons.

Two of my soldiers who will accompany you will also have night vision devices, but we don't have enough radios for you to take one."

"Radios? What might that be? It is not a piece of kit we carry."

"Don't worry. I am sure you will do well with the night vision devices."

Platoon Sergeant Jackson has identified Specialist Costanza and PFC Hunt as the two who will accompany Sergeant Smyth on the dash to Jalalabad. Both Costanza and Hunt are fitted with NODs. Hunt has an M320 grenade launcher mounted under his M4 and is carrying twenty 40mm high explosive rounds.

One of the spare M4s from the helicopter is handed to Sergeant Smyth. PFC Hunt goes over the weapon, cocking, using the selector switch, and inserting and pulling out the magazine. Smyth makes three dry runs with the M4 and declares,

"My, what a simple weapon to use. No loading of each shot and being able to shoot many times before reloading is too good."

Before he can continue, Platoon Sergeant Jackson briefs them on their mission, and the three move with Sergeant Jackson to where the two lieutenants are seated around a warming fire.

Lieutenant Wilkinson greets them, "Gentlemen, Lieutenant Short and I agree that it is imperative that the garrison at Jalalabad know of our dire straits and send a relief column as soon as possible. We suspect that the garrison may have given us up for lost. You are to contact the garrison and convince them to send relief as soon as possible."

Lieutenant Short adds, "Sergeant Smyth has traveled this road before. We trust his ability to get the three of you to Jalalabad before morning. Costanza and Hunt, avoid contact if possible, but be prepared to rain some steel on anyone who gets in your way. You three have the only working night vision devices available. Use them well."

The three nod and shoulder their weapons. As they move outside the perimeter and east to Jalalabad, Sergeant Jackson shakes his head,

"Damn, I wish we could give them a radio. They are really on their own."

Shortly after Smyth, Costanza, and Hunt leave, Doc Kramer approaches the lieutenants.

"Gentlemen, I have had to put three more soldiers into the wagons. They cannot walk another step with the severe frostbite they have suffered. Lieutenant Wilkinson, I have moved Captain Souter's body to the outside of the wagon. We needed the room for those who cannot walk. I have tended to the two horses pulling the wagons, but they, too, are on their last legs."

"Miss Kramer, thank you for all you are doing for the soldiers. I know Captain Souter would gladly give up his space for his soldiers."

# Chapter Ten: Scramble to Jalalabad for Relief

Smyth, Costanza, and Hunt have now moved more than a kilometer from the main group. Smyth holds up his hand, indicating a halt. He whispers to the other two, "Do you see the fires in the near distance?"

Constanza replies, "Yes, but are they in our way?"

"I believe not," says Smyth, "but we need be careful in covering the ground between the fires. The tribesmen may not be able to see as well as we with the magic glasses, but if we come close enough, they can hear us."

"How much further, do you think, Sergeant Smyth?" says Hunter. "The longer I stand, the colder I get."

"Let's move quickly and carefully for the next mile or so," says Smyth. "I suspect that if the garrison at Jalalabad is under siege, the tribesmen around those fires are the ones laying the siege."

The three move quickly and carefully until they are surprised by a shout from their left. Although they cannot understand what was said, it was clearly a warning. Just as quickly, the sound of muskets being fired in multiple directions crashes against the rocky landscape.

Hunter is the first to react and fires a three-round burst from his M4 at the flash closest to him. His firing alerts the groups nearest them, and they concentrate fire on the three. Costanza places a 40mm grenade in the midst of the closest group and follows with two well-aimed shots from his M4. The tribesmen continue to fire wildly, and Smyth, Costanza, and Hunter push faster toward the break in the terrain ahead.

Sergeant Smyth, out of breath and staggering, grabs Constanza and pulls him to the ground.

"Lad, I must rest for a bit. These old legs are not what they once were. I believe we have confused the tribesmen once again."

Constanza and Hunt sweep the area around them and cannot see any tribesmen moving. The dark night and cloud cover keep the three hidden from those who cannot see in the dark. Hunt pulls out a hand warmer packet, breaks the chemical vial inside, and hands it to Smyth.

"Stick this inside your jacket and place your hands on it. Keeping your core warm will help you recover quickly."

"Your magic kit is all the more welcome in this wretched cold.

Although the three can hear tribesmen talking in the distance, they are not moving in their direction. The three rise and continue their trek to the garrison at Jalalabad. The glow on the horizon must be Jalalabad, as the sun will not rise for another hour. With this as encouragement, the three pick up their pace.

The group of three is within sight of the town of Jalalabad as the sun breaks over the horizon. Smyth turns to the other two and says, " Lads, we'd best wait for better daylight. We don't need to have our boys on the wall mistaking us for attackers.

## Ghost Soldiers of Gandamak

As Lieutenant Wilkinson's column exits the draw, Sergeant Smyth, Specialist Constanza, and PFC Hunt, a mile ahead, crest a large hill and see the town of Jalalabad below. They also see large groups of tribesmen gathered between them and the town. Smyth turns to Costanza, "Mr. Costanza, the garrison is still there as I see the Union Jack flying above the citadel in the middle of the town. Do you have any thoughts as to how we can part the groups in front and make the town?"

Costanza turns to Smyth, "Sergeant, we can blast our way through them, but the numbers may make our firepower less effective at close range. When we are within 400 yards, I will start dropping grenades on them, and that should give us a path through. Should some of them get too close, Hunt has a couple of frag grenades he can throw that will also give us some time to move. When he yells, 'grenade," we must hit the ground and lie flat. Those standing anywhere near the grenade will be killed. Once we have exhausted the grenades, a little rapid rifle fire should convey to them that we are coming through. This is your chance to use the M4 you are carrying. If, by chance, you have selected rapid fire, please keep it pointed at the bad guys."

"All right, chaps. This is the only way into the town. Let us proceed," says Smyth.

The groups of tribesmen on the south side of town appear to be focused on the town itself and its imposing walls. Occasionally, they fire a shot or two at a soldier manning the walls. The walls surrounding the town are heavy stone and almost twelve feet high. Two very heavy log gates bar a single entry. The musket rounds make no difference while chipping away some of the wood.

Smyth, Costanza, and Hunt walk slowly down the hillside and are unnoticed until they are about 500 yards from the nearest group of tribesmen. Costanza has a grenade loaded and fires at his immediate front. The explosion knocks down the first five figures in the group. Two quick two-round bursts from Hunt leave another four tribesmen on the ground. There is now much confusion in the various groups. Two more grenades explode in the tight groups, and more tribesmen either lie in the snow or are dragging themselves away from the blasts. Costanza now launches grenades to the rear of the two groups now separated by the bodies ahead of the three. Costanza, Smyth, and Hunt now fire two-round bursts from their M4s directly into the groups on their left and right. A group of five attempts to get behind them. Hunt sees them before they can get close and yells, "Grenade," and throws a fragmentation grenade into the middle of the group of five. The three hit the ground as the grenade blast explodes in the middle of the group, eliminating the threat.

The three are now beyond the groups of tribesmen and approach the town gate. Sergeant Smyth calls to one of the soldiers on the wall,

"Open the gate, you bastards. Can't ye tell we are fighting men?"

As the gate swings ponderously on its hinges, musket fire begins to hit close to Hunt. He returns fire, and the two or three who attempted to fire on him are now in the snow. Costanza drops one more 40mm grenade on the group of tribesmen as the three enter the gate, and it swings shut behind them.

The three are down on one knee, catching their breath, when a uniformed individual strides toward them. Resplendent in the uniform of a Guards officer, he surveys the three and asks,

"Who are you, and what weapons did you use on the tribesmen at our walls?"

Recognizing the officer, Sergeant Smyth stands at attention, salutes, and replies, "Color Sergeant Alex Smyth, Sir, First Company, 44th Foot."

"My God, man, we had given you up for dead. Are you three the only survivors?"

"No, sir," says Smyth, "we are but the advance of the much larger column. The 44th Foot is much the worse for wear, sir, and they will be along later this morning. Had it not been for the Americans joining us at Gandamak, I fear that it would have been the end of the regiment. We must go out in force and assist their march here. I fear that without assistance, they may not be able to make the journey. Many of the soldiers are wounded or disabled from the cold."

The officer now turns to Costanza and Hunt, "Gentlemen, I am Leftenant Colonel Gordon James, the Commandant of this garrison. Welcome, and thank you for assisting. I find your uniform and weapons very strange. I watched the mayhem that you inflicted on the tribesmen that allowed you to reach the gate. Can you provide the same fires when we send a relief party to the approaching column?"

Always ready to provide a wisecrack, Costanza looks at the immaculate uniform and decides to play it straight. "Yes, sir, we can and will gladly accompany the relief so that we may rejoin our own unit with the larger column."

The colonel turns and calls, "Sergeant Major, I want a company ready to march in a half hour. One day's rations and a full complement of rifle ammunition. Meanwhile, I suggest the three of you get inside, have a hot drink, and be ready to join the relief column."

As the three walk to the barracks, guided by the Sergeant Major, Smyth's tattered uniform draws only slightly more stares from the assembled British soldiers than the uniforms and weapons carried by Smyth, Constanza, and Hunt.

Smyth, Costanza, and Hunt quickly down the warm oatmeal a cook has prepared for them and sip the hot tea laced with brandy. Rejuvenated, the three leave the cookhouse and join the column, preparing to leave Jalalabad.

Smyth approaches the young officer in charge, "Sir, if I may. My two companions and I can part the tribesmen more efficiently than our bayonets. I suggest you let us lead the way to the rest of the 44th Foot."

The young officer mounts his horse and gestures to the other two mounted soldiers, "We shall follow the two Americans out of the town. Keep watch on your flanks as we proceed."

Costanza checks his vest and realizes he has only five 40mm grenades remaining. Checking with Hunt, they have five magazines each of 5.56 ammunition and five M67 fragmentation grenades. They look at each other and realize they are not as well armed as they were on the approach to the town.

Costanza turns to the officer, "Sir, Hunt and I will lead the column. We will make certain the tribesmen do not interfere with us."

"So be it," says the young officer as he calls for the gates to be opened and the soldiers on the wall to warn of any tribesmen approaching.

Costanza and Hunt slip through the now-open gates and find far fewer tribesmen in the open area they had just traversed. Those they can see are keeping a great distance from them.

"Sergeant Smyth, do you think they have learned a lesson or two about attacking us?" said Hunt.

"Aye, lad. They have learned a lesson, but they are a crafty bunch and will wait for the right time to attack, and that is not now."

# Chapter Eleven: The Slow March

While Smyth, Costanza and Hunt have reached the garrison at Jalalabad, Lieutenant Short and Wilkinson recognize that letting the soldiers stay too long in one place is a sure recipe for disaster. In this cold, they must keep moving. The few warming fires have helped, but movement is imperative. Lieutenant Wilkinson calls for Corporal Sethewick.

"Sethewick, we must be moving. Have every soldier warm as best they can and be ready to march on the hour."

Lieutenant Short calls Sergeant Bishop.

"Scott, see if any more hot packs can be distributed to the British soldiers. We need to get moving at dawn, which is less than an hour from now."

"Sir, we have shared our last hot pack and our last MRE. Our guys are down to the sundry packs in the MREs, and if we don't get some water pretty soon, it could get worse."

Lieutenant Short turns to Lieutenant Wilkinson, "James, we must reach Jalalabad tomorrow morning if any of us are going to survive this march."

The column that begins to move at dawn is ragged and slow. Many American soldiers are supporting British soldiers who can barely walk. Their tattered uniforms and blanket-wrapped heads are testimony to a long and difficult march from Kabul. Few in the column walk unaided. Specialist Turbin, the largest member of the platoon at six feet five inches, has his M249 light machine gun across his back and has two British soldiers with their arms around his neck. As Lieutenant Short acknowledges Turbin, he smiles and thinks to himself,

"What great soldiers and great human beings these men are. I pray we will be able to save them and our British allies."

Ahead of the column, Sergeant Bishop and Corporal Glenn watch the terrain ahead of them and often scan the hills with binoculars. They heard the gunfire earlier in the morning and wondered how Smyth, Costanza, and Hunter made it.

"Bishop, what do you think? Can we get these guys to Jalalabad? They are in bad shape, and I think those wagons are going to break any minute."

The horse pulling the lead wagon drops over at that moment and lies quivering in the snow.

"Dammit, Glenn. Did you just have to say that? I hope the lieutenants have something up their sleeves because it doesn't look like any of those in the wagon are going to walk anywhere."

The two lieutenants now have a dilemma. They are less than two miles from Jalalabad, but many British soldiers cannot travel. They also have no idea if the lead party of Smyth, Costanza, and Hunt have made it to the garrison at Jalalabad. If they did make it and there is a relief column enroute, how long would it be before they arrive? And will the soldiers in the worst condition succumb to their injuries before support is provided?

"James, I believe we have no choice but to split the column. Leave enough security here with the wounded and the sick, and those that can make it to the garrison at Jalalabad leave soon. Should they meet a relief column enroute, they can direct them to the location of those staying here."

"Roger, it will be difficult to leave anyone. Who will remain for the wounded and sick?"

"James, I suggest that ten of my soldiers act as your security on the road to Jalalabad. I will remain here with the rest of my soldiers and our medic. We can provide sufficient security and hopefully medical assistance for as long as necessary."

"There are ten of my soldiers in the two carts and another five that cannot walk. We shall move as quickly as possible to Jalalabad and put forth our best effort to have a relief column back to you as soon as possible."

"James, we cannot ask for more. I will ask Sergeant Bishop to go with your group and provide the security you will need."

Sergeant Bishop recalls the members of his squad and gives them a quick update on what they will be doing. He and his squad fan out in front of the slow-moving column of British soldiers, with Lieutenant Wilkinson in the lead. As dawn breaks on the horizon, the soldiers recognize that Jalalabad is just over that horizon, which adds some quickness to their pace. The stark, white mountains in the background now reflect the sunlight and give an unworldly glow to the column.

Sergeant Wilson has rounded up his squad and assigned sectors of responsibility for each of the ten soldiers around the perimeter of the two wagons and the British soldiers huddled around their warming fires. The wagon that lost its horse is soon stripped of wood, and another warming fire gives more relief to those who cannot walk. Specialist Kramer makes her way from the small groups around the two fires and the soldiers in the remaining wagon, checking on the condition of the soldiers. Having completed her rounds, Kramer goes to Lieutenant Short,

"Sir, these guys are on their last canteen of water. Some have only had some of our MREs in the last two days, and I don't have any more antibiotics to treat the infections. I don't think I can do anything more for them."

"Doc, I know it doesn't get any better," says Lieutenant Short, "but your presence seems to greatly affect their morale. You have made a big difference as a trained medic and a woman."

Kramer wryly smiles, "Lieutenant, I don't see how I helped their morale. Mine is lower than dog shit. I can't believe we should have been home two days ago."

Sergeant Bishop has no trouble following the trail of the three who left earlier that morning. He notices that the three have hit the ground and lay prone in the snow on more than one occasion. A couple of brass casings from an M4 provide the reason. So far, they have not seen or heard any tribesmen. As they approach a break in the terrain, he thinks, "This is a good place for an ambush," and calls to Corporal Glenn, "Glenn hit both sides of that draw with a grenade. I don't want any surprises on this last part."

Corporal Glenn quickly fires one grenade on the draw's north side and another on the south side. The explosions do not draw any tribesmen, and the sounds of the two explosions bring Lieutenant Wilkinson up to the leading element.

"Gentlemen, has there been a sighting of tribesmen? Did you fire on them?"

"Lieutenant, I was just being careful. If we were going to be ambushed, that draw would be a good place for it to happen. We drew no fire and did not see anyone."

Wilkinson's relief is apparent as they approach the draw and can see Smyth's, Constanza's, and Hunt's trail headed east.

Smyth, Costanza, and Hunt are now leading the soldiers in the relief column across the hilltop. As they crest the hill, they see the group of British and American soldiers less than a mile away moving slowly toward them. Between the two columns are at least a hundred tribesmen. Some appear and reappear among the rocks and crevices, others dashing between cuts in the hills. Very few are in the open, and all seem to be waiting for them.

Smyth turns to the lieutenant in charge of the relief column: "Leftenant, it appears we have a welcoming party for each of us. You may notice that some of the same soldiers who accompanied me are now leading the column moving to us. I suggest we let the Americans take the lead in pushing the tribesmen away."

"What Americans?" says the lieutenant.

"The two you see in front of us and the dozen or so leading the other column."

Lieutenant Wilkinson and Sergeant Bishop see the same large number of tribesmen as Smyth. Bishop says to Wilkinson,

"Lieutenant, let me and my guys prepare for the rest of the way. I think some well-placed grenades and rifle fire will discourage any attacks on us or the relief column we see in the distance."

"Sergeant Bishop, I have great confidence in you and your soldiers. What is the plan?"

"I will move my two grenadiers closer to the front of the column and have the machine guns with them. As soon as the grenades land in the midst of the largest groups, I will have the machine guns place direct fire on the remaining groups. We should all move to the next hilltop at the impact of the first grenades. From there, we can join up with the relief column."

"Sergeant Bishop, make it so."

# Ghost Soldiers of Gandamak

Sergeant Bishop places his two grenadiers and two machine gunners at the head of the column. He instructs the grenadiers to put two rounds into the two largest groups. The machine gunners are to follow the grenades with direct fire on any tribesmen they observe. Lieutenant Wilkinson has Corporal Sethewick pass the word down the column that the British soldiers are to quick march as soon as the first explosion is heard. The remaining six American soldiers are now on the column's flanks and prepared to repel any flanking attacks.

Sergeant Bishop gives the command to fire. Quickly, four 40mm grenades are launched and fall into the largest of the four groups of tribesmen. As the column surges forward, machine gun fire from the two M249s blasts any tribesman who shows his face. The carnage in the rocky terrain is even more than Bishop could hope for. The grenades blast the groups of tribesmen, and the shards of rocks blown into them by the grenades. The accurate machine gun fire has decimated those closest to the advancing column. Soon, the unwounded tribesmen scatter north and south among the hills. The dead and dying tribesmen lay in the snow where they fell as the two columns meet where an ambush had been planned.

The two British officers meet and introduce themselves.

"I am Leftenant Jones-Parham of her majesties Irish Guard Regiment."

"It's my pleasure, Leftenant. I am Leftenant Wilkinson of Her Majesty's 44th Foot. I believe we met once as Sandhurst or Cambridge, did we not?"

"We did, and I remember well that your Father, the Earl of Wessex, was also a member of the regiment. Are you now the Earl of Wessex?

"I am Leftenant, as my father passed away two years ago."

"Then we are ever so glad that you and others from the 44th Foot have survived. We knew that you were ordered to the Jalalabad garrison from Kabul, but we did not know how bad that march would be."

"Leftenant, we had to leave our most serious wounded and disabled behind. The rest of the Americans provide security, but we must go to them as quickly as possible. Do you have any transport available at the garrison.?

"We do," said Jones-Parham, "I will have two mounted Guardsmen ride back to the garrison and fetch two wagons. I assume that will be sufficient?"

"It will," assures Wilkinson, "but we should proceed with the relief force and let the wagons catch us."

# Chapter Twelve: The Final March

Lieutenant Short and his small group of infantrymen providing security for the disabled and wounded British soldiers have only been sporadically harassed by tribesmen. The few dead and wounded tribesmen who attempted to attack have been quickly taken from the blood-stained snow. Doc Kramer has stabilized the wounded in the remaining wagon. The remaining horse has collapsed from the cold and the lack of food. There is no moving the wagon or the wounded.

Short is now faced with the problem of how to get back to their time and place. The location of the helicopter crash and the hasty graves of those killed in the crash are about ten miles south-southwest of their current location. If and when the relief column from Jalalabad arrives, consolidating his soldiers and returning to the crash site seems the best alternative. The difference this time is that they all know the route and a ten mile movement is challenging but doable.

As daylight begins to fade in the snow-covered hills, one of the soldiers exclaims, "Here they come. I see Costanza and Hunt. It's a pretty large unit following them."

Lieutenant Short is relieved to see his two soldiers alive and well. He is also surprised to see three mounted soldiers and two wagons pulled by a pair of horses. His surprise increases when he notices Lieutenant Wilkinson is on one of the horses.

When the relief column closes on the small contingent around the disabled and wounded, a weak cheer greets them. Short reaches

Lieutenant Wilkinson as he dismounts, "James, I see you were successful in reaching the garrison at Jalalabad."

"Roger, it could not have been done without your soldiers destroying the tribesmen at every encounter. May I introduce Leftenant George Jones-Parham, the officer in charge of the relief?"

"Glad to meet you, Lieutenant. We had every confidence that Lieutenant Wilkinson would make it to Jalalabad."

"It is my pleasure, Leftenant Short. His lordship tells me you have had bad luck with your transport. I must say that the weapons you and your soldiers employ are a sight to behold."

"I am not sure what you just said; who is his lordship?"

Jones-Parham smiles and turns to Wilkinson, "I assume you have not shared with your American counterpart that you are the Earl of Wessex?"

"I did but did not think it relevant at the time," replies Wilkinson with a smile.

Now slightly confused, Short turns to Wilkinson and says, "James, I don't think it would have made any difference. I am just glad to know that we could support you and your regiment."

"Roger, thank you again for coming to our aid. We shall not forget the role you played on the trek to Jalalabad. May I suggest that we move at first light to the garrison?"

"James, I need to discuss our next efforts to return to our time and place with my soldiers. There is no guarantee that we can, but moving to Jalalabad and becoming immersed in the town will make that harder."

"I understand, Roger. We will support whatever decision you make."

As the soldiers gather around their warming fires, Lieutenant Short sits with Platoon Sergeant Jackson.

"Wil, I am unsure how we return to our time and place. I believe it would be more difficult if we were to join the Brits in Jalalabad."

"Lieutenant, I agree. If nothing else, our chances are better if we could get back to the crash site."

"OK, as soon as the relief party is prepared to leave in the morning, we will give the tribesmen one last taste of Army firepower and head back to the crash site."

Lieutenant Short finds Lieutenants Wilkinson and Jones-Parham as they supervise the transfer of wounded and disabled to the new wagons.

"James, we must return to our crash site as soon as you are prepared to leave. Our only hope of returning to our time and unit is at the crash site. Before leaving, we are going to drop major hurt on the tribesmen we see."

"Roger, I understand. I hope we can return to Jalalabad as easily as we left with the additional soldiers from the garrison."

The night passes uneventfully as the American and British soldiers endure another night in the bleak, cold Afghan winter. At first light, Lieutenant Short brings his squad leaders and the senior weapons squad member to his fire.

"I want to tell you all that you have done an amazing job supporting the Brits. I am sure they would not have survived otherwise. Our task is now to return to the crash site and wait for rescue. We will drop some hurt on the nearest tribesmen and head southwest to our destination. The Brits should not have trouble returning to Jalalabad without our assistance. Sergeant Bishop, please recover the M4 from Sergeant Smyth. I know he would like it as a memento, but leaving it with them might change too much history."

Platoon Sergeant Jackson has the 60mm mortar crew prepared to drop mortar rounds on the groups of tribesmen gathered in the nearby hills. They have learned that where they see one or two, these are scouts, and the main body is close. With unerring accuracy, the 60mm mortar crew expends the remaining twenty rounds carried by the platoon.

As the sound of the first explosion, Lieutenant Jones-Parham races to Lieutenant Wilkinson.

"Your lordship, what type of ordnance do these American soldiers possess? They seem to be able to blast the tribesmen anywhere they appear."

"George, they have much-improved munitions that we have never seen. I feel certain our march back to Jalalabad will be much the better for it."

The two parties face opposite directions as the noon-time sun washes over the surrounding mountains. The remnants of the 44th Foot and the company from the garrison at Jalalabad prepare to move east. The twenty-five soldiers of the 3rd Platoon, A Company, 2/22 Infantry look west toward the low mountains where their Chinook crashed four days ago.

Two thoughts cross each American soldier's mind, "How will we get back? And "I am glad we were able to help the British soldiers survive."

As the two groups move, Lieutenant Short and Lieutenant Wilkinson meet for the last time.

"Roger, we would not have survived were it not for you and your soldiers. Your contribution will forever be remembered in the history of the regiment."

"James, I think I speak for all the soldiers. We are grateful to have been here when we were needed. As soldiers, we all know that we fight better together. God bless you and your soldiers. May they all recover."

# Ghost Soldiers of Gandamak

The two groups move toward their destinations in the dim sunshine of another winter day in Afghanistan. One group hopes to return to their time and place, while the other rejoices in being alive and able to carry on.

Lieutenant Wilkinson looks at the twenty-five American soldiers moving swiftly west and wonders what he will tell members of the regiment in the future. The once proud regiment is now a shadow of its former glory, and the survivors have encountered soldiers from the future. How can they explain what they saw to those who have not experienced it? To paraphrase Sergeant Smyth, "Not bloody likely."

# Epilogue

*Immediate Release*

**DoD Identifies Army Casualties**

**Jan. 20, 2023**

The Department of Defense announced today the loss of thirty-three soldiers supporting Operation Inherent Resolve. A transport CH-47, carrying thirty soldiers from A Company, 2/22 Infantry, 1BCT, 10th Mountain Division, and three crew members from the 10th Aviation Brigade, was found in the mountains south of Jalalabad. The aircraft was reported overdue at Kandahar Airbase on January 12. An intense air and ground search was made. As a result of that search, it was determined that there were no survivors. All casualties have been recovered.

A full list of the casualties will be available once all families and next of kin have been contacted.

For more information regarding the casualty loss, members of the media may contact Lt. Col. Jason Aldie, Chief of Public Information, U.S. Army Public Affairs Office, Fort Drum, NY, at 999-570-8337, Mobile 999-622-3654, or by email at Jason.aldie.mil@army.mil.

# Ghost Soldiers of Gandamak

## Last Stand of the 44<sup>th</sup> Foot[2]

On 13 January 1842, British forces were defeated by Afghan tribesmen in General Elphinstone's army retreat from Kabul, during which the last survivors of the force—two officers and fifty British soldiers of the 44th East Essex Regiment—were killed in a last stand near the village of Gandamak. Traces of weapons and equipment from the battle could be seen in the 1970s, and as late as 2010, the bones of the dead still covered the hillside.

---

[2] Painting by William Barnes Wollem can be seen at the Essex Regiment Museum, Chelmsford Museum, Moulsham Street, Chelmsford, CM2 9AQ

# Cast of Characters

| 10th Mountain Division, 1st BCT | 2nd Bn, 22nd Inf, A Co, 3rd platoon + | 44th Foot | |
|---|---|---|---|
| US soldiers | position | British soldiers | position |
| LT Roger Williams Short | Plat Ldr 3rd plat, USMA 2020 | James Richard Wilkinson | Lieutenant of the 44th Foot, Earl of Essex |
| SFC Wilfred Jackson | Plat Sgt 3rd plat, 2nd tour in Afghan | Captain Thomas Alexander Souter | Senior officer on scene wounded |
| SGT Ron Wilson | 1st sqd ldr | Color SergeantT Alex Smyth | Senior NCO on scene |
| SGT Scott Bishop | 2nd sqd ldr | Corporal Sethewick | Sr Corporal |
| Corporal Peter Garcia | Tm Ldr weapons sqd | Corporal Smithers | Jr Corporal |
| Corporal Michael Glenn | Tm Ldr | Private Jones | Severe frostbite |
| Spec Turbin | 1st sqd MG | Private Withers | Severe frostbite |
| Spec Waters | 1st Sqd rifleman | Private Hawkins | Severe frostbite |

# Ghost Soldiers of Gandamak

| | | | |
|---|---|---|---|
| Spec Leo Costanza | 2$^{nd}$ sqd grenadier | Private Wilkins | Wounded unable to travel |
| Specialist Sharon Kramer | Plat medic, only female | Private Scoggins | Wounded unable to travel |
| Spec Crosby | Wise ass 2$^{nd}$ sqd MG | Private Maggard | Wounded unable to travel |
| PFC Hunt | 2$^{nd}$ Sqd grenadier | Private Stipf | Wounded unable to travel |
| SP Lumbert | 2$^{nd}$ sqd rifleman | Private Paxton | Wounded unable to travel |
| Spec Zegan | 1$^{st}$ sqd rifleman | | |
| Spec Dixon | 2$^{nd}$ sqd rifleman | | |
| Spec Thompson | 2$^{nd}$ sqd rifleman | | |
| PFC Jones | 2$^{nd}$ sqd rifleman | | |

# Weapons and Equipment

British 44<sup>th</sup> Foot

60 mm mortar

US 10<sup>th</sup> Mountain Division

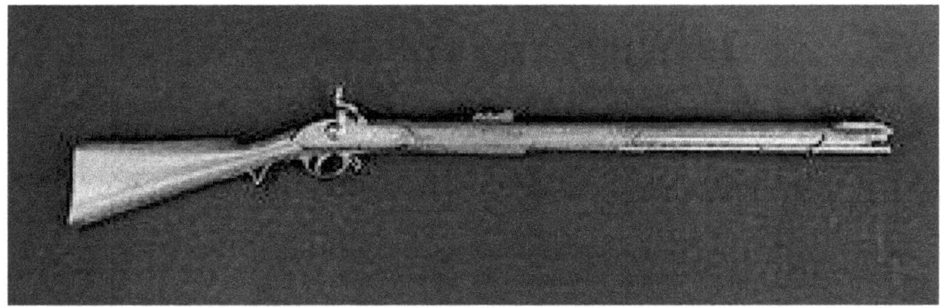

Brunswick Rifle .704 caliber
muzzle-loading percussion rifle

M4 carbine 5.56 mm

M110 Sniper rifle, 7.62mm

M249 Light MG 5.56mm

M4 Carbine w/M320 Grenade Launcher

M67 Hand grenade

# About The Author

Dr. Hennessey served in the United States Army for over 28 years in successively responsible leadership positions, retiring as a Colonel. During that time, he received multiple awards for distinguished service.

After retiring from the Army in 1993, Hennessey was appointed the University Chief of Staff at George Mason University. Until his retirement in 2013, he remained a teaching faculty member, teaching undergraduate and graduate-level courses in public management, policy, and governance.

Since 2005, Dr. Hennessey has served as the founder and president of Hennessey Management Consulting, LLC. This consultancy works with clients in the federal and state governments, as well as the higher education community. He is an avid reader and writer. Dr. Hennessey and his wife, Barbara, reside in Leesburg, Virginia.